the Sun and the Moon

Brian D. McClure

Illustrated by Buddy Plumlee

UNIVERSAL FLAG PUBLISHING • LISLE ILLINOIS

My dedication is to you, in honor of the
great gifts you bring to our world!

Thank you for who you are!

Brian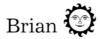

This is a story about you and me, but for the protection of us...

Hmmn let me see... I have it... here we go...

It happened one day right out of the blue, the Sun told the Moon he was tired and through. "What do you mean," the Moon asked the Sun, "that would be the end of everything, and that wouldn't be fun."

"What do you know!" grunted the Sun, "your reflected light isn't useful to anyone." The Moon got mad and called the Sun a jerk, and that was the beginning of all of the murk. The argument continued for quite some time, they called each other names that sure didn't rhyme.

For you and me, it is easy to see, that the Sun and the Moon were acting just like humans. When humans get mad they act out of fear, if you're in the middle, it's wise to stay clear. Sometimes they yell and throw things and scream, and that's when you wish it was only a dream.

For the Sun and the Moon, this argument was their first. For all those on earth it was certainly the worst. The Sun stopped shining as he yelled at the Moon, things sure got ugly, and it wasn't over soon. They both walked out on their responsibilities that day. They affected the earth in a very big way.

The first thing that happened when the argument began was the loss of all light, all over the land. The sky went black in the snap of a finger, not one trace of light was able to linger. That was just the start, of the havoc that ensued, things only got worse as the argument brewed.

The Moon yelled back at the Sun in a rage, while the earth was on course, for another ice age. Besides the loss of light, the earth's heat was all gone; soon the planet would awaken, to a new frozen dawn. As the temperatures dropped the crops were frozen in place, it was a terrible disaster affecting the whole human race.

11

The water froze first along with the land; everything became solid, including the sand. Animals and insects were iced in a flash; everything resulting from the Sun and Moons' clash. Things on the earth were looking quite bleak; the planet would be gone in less than a week. If the Sun and the Moon were not back by then, all life would be lost, until who knows when.

As the Sun and the Moon continued to fight, neither was aware of the poor earth's plight. For them it was impossible to see anything clear, the only thing they focused on was all of their fear.

Now let's stop the story for a moment or two, there are a few things about humans; I would like to share with you.

While most humans believe that they are angry and mad, it's really just their fears that they always have had. Fears linger inside, completely hidden from view, awaiting the opportunity to shout and spew. The more fears one has, the harder the fight, it's a very tough thing when you need to be right.

Fears cause problems in every new day. They are the reason for wars, and crimes that don't pay. At the root of it all are the feelings of less; which causes great pain and much undue stress. These feelings remain for the most part asleep; they are hidden inside of us, and buried very deep.

Here is how fear works inside of us.

Along comes a word or an action of another... it even could come from our sister or our brother... our feelings kick up as fast as can be... and the next thing we know... we are so mad... we can't see... we react in a flash... we scream and we lash... we shout and we pout... we blame without doubt.

Now, let's get back to our story...

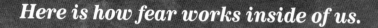

We left off where... the Sun and the Moon continued to fight, neither was aware of the poor earths plight. For them it was impossible to see anything clear, the only thing they focused on was all of their fear.

"You called me a jerk," the Sun yelled at the Moon, "I won't forget that you little baboon."

"What?" the Moon screamed in reply, "you called me useless; you're less than a fly."

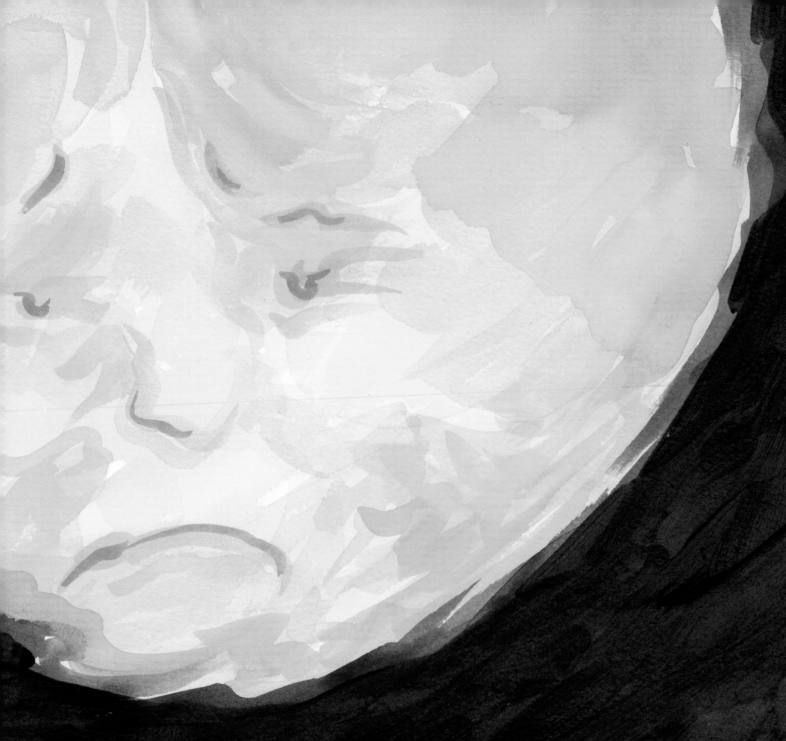

As the Sun and Moon continued to fight, they finally reached a point where they didn't feel right. It happened like that, in the blink of an eye, as their anger turned to sadness, and they needed to know why! Why had they both continued along? Why had it been so difficult, to admit they were wrong?

They had hurt themselves by getting so mad, there was a way to fix that, which wasn't so bad! It was at that very point that they remembered their truth, it was one that had escaped them through all of their youth.

Can you guess the truth they remembered?

Here is a clue...

The Sun and the Moon are connected to both me and you!

We Are Connected To All!

When we call each other names to feel better inside, we hurt ourselves, in the name of our pride... not only that... we are connected to all... we affect many more... when we scream and we brawl... most we don't see, so we remain unaware... that doesn't mean... that we shouldn't care!

And so... with their awareness of connection... let's see how the Sun and the Moon changed their direction!

All of a sudden, right out of the blue, the Sun told the Moon he was tired and through. The Moon thought for a second and started to laugh, he apologized to the Sun on everyone's behalf. The Sun said, "No!" "I apologize to you, if you were not a part of me, what would I do?" "I have acted foolishly and I've hurt many too. Please forgive me Moon, and let's start anew."

Just about that time they noticed a sound, without even thinking they both looked around. For the first time, since their quarrel had begun, they saw the earth suffering as a result of no sun. In that instant, they were both as shocked as could be, they had no idea; they had caused such a spree.

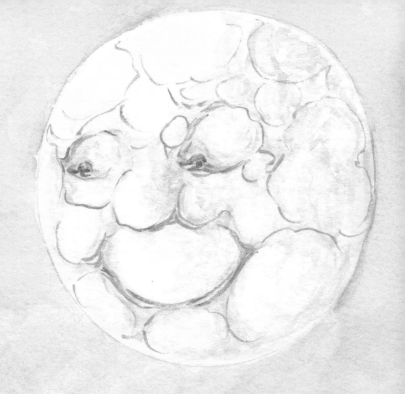

They went back to their jobs in the blink of an eye; they
had no time to waste, for the whole earth could die. The light
hit the planet in no time at all. For all of the earth, it was a
very close call.

Slowly but surely, a great thaw took place, in the end it
saved the whole human race. The Moon was able to stir up a
breeze, the waves were returned to the lakes and the seas.
The animals and insects had freedom once more, it was
certainly a gift that was hard to ignore. The crops started new
growth, with the return of the light. Everything basked in a
feeling of delight.

Everywhere on earth there vibrated a sound; it came from everything, from the sky to the ground. It was the same sound that was heard by the Sun and the Moon, the very sound that saved the earth, from its certain doom.

Can you guess the sound?

I'll give you a clue; the same sound vibrates, directly from you.

A Prayer

In each new moment, everything sends out a prayer, it comes from inside, and is sent everywhere. Sometimes it's a prayer of gratitude for all gifts, but all prayers change with external shifts. There is one thing that is constant and will always be true, that is the prayer, in all that we do. Makes no difference what that may be, a prayer always vibrates from you and me.

And now for You! Before you go, there are a few things
the Sun, the Moon and I would like you to know.

You are a Great Gift to the World!

You are Loved every second of every day!

You are One with everything there is!

We are looking forward to seeing you soon.
Thank you for reading, "Our Story!"

The Beginning

33

The Universal Flag represents our connection
with everyone and everything that exists in our world.

To learn more about our Universal Flag,
please visit us at: www.UniversalFlag.com